Topic: Health   **Subtopic:** Fitness

Notes to Parents and Teachers:

As a child becomes more familiar reading books, it is important for him/her to rely on and use reading strategies more independently to help figure out words they do not know.

REMEMBER: PRAISE IS A GREAT MOTIVATOR!

Here are some praise points for beginning readers:

• I saw you get your mouth ready to say the first letter of that word.
• I like the way you used the picture to help you figure out that word.
• I noticed that you saw some sight words you knew how to read!

Book Ends for the Reader!

Here are some reminders before reading the text:

• Point to each word you read to make it match what you say.
• Use the picture for help.
• Look at and say the first letter sound of the word.
• Look for sight words that you know how to read in the story.
• Think about the story to see what word might make sense.

Words to Know Before You Read

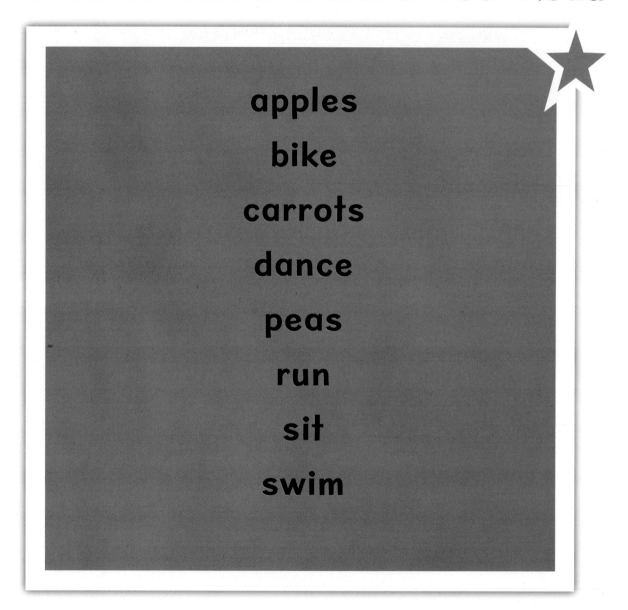

apples

bike

carrots

dance

peas

run

sit

swim

Ready Readers

COUCH POTATO

A Story About Making Healthy Choices

NPOSSIBLE CLASSROOM LIBRARIES
N
COX'S CREEK ELEMENTARY SCHOOL

BY
KATY DUFFIELD

ILLUSTRATED BY
JUNISSA BIANDA

COUCH POTATO

A Story About Making Healthy Choices

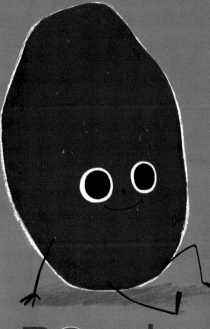

By Katy Duffield

Illustrated by
Junissa Bianda

Rourke
Educational Media
rourkeeducationalmedia.com

Spud is a couch potato.

4

Couch potatoes don't want to move.
They just want to sit, sit, sit.

"Let's run!" the carrot calls.

"Not today," Spud says.

"Let's bike!" the bananas call.

"No way," Spud says.

"Let's swim!" the apples call.

"Maybe Tuesday," Spud says.

Spud doesn't bike. Spud doesn't run. Spud doesn't swim.

Spud sits.

But then...Spud hears something.

And it's something he can't resist!

"Let's dance!" the peas call.

And this time...

Spud doesn't say,
"Not today."

He doesn't say,
"No way."

He doesn't say, "Maybe Tuesday."

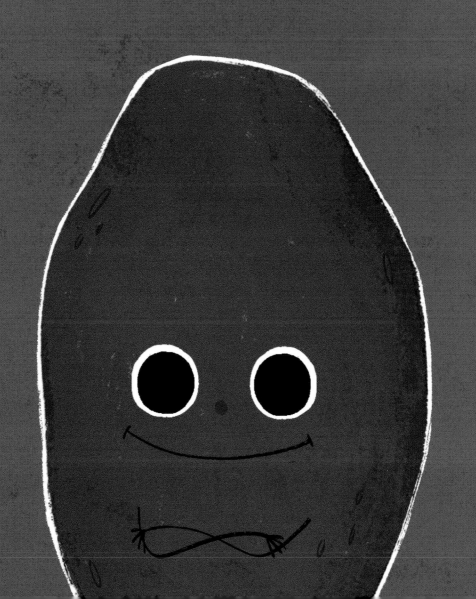

Spud says, "OKAY!"

And he dance-dance-dances the day away.

Book Ends for the Reader

I know...

1. What does Spud want to do in the beginning of the story?

2. What do the carrots want to do?

3. What do the apples want to do?

I think...

1. Is it important to exercise? Why or why not?

2. Did Spud make a healthy choice in the end?

3. What are some healthy choices you made today?

Book Ends for the Reader

What happened in this book?

Look at each picture and talk about what happened in the story.

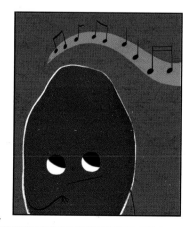

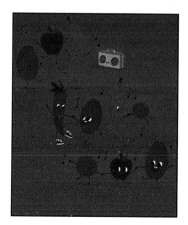

About the Author

Katy Duffield is an author from Florida. Katy is NOT a couch potato. She likes to walk, bike, do yoga, and play golf.

About the Illustrator

Junissa Bianda is an illustrator from Indonesia with a passion for art! Rarely do you see her without a colored pencil and a sketchbook in her grasp.

Library of Congress PCN Data

Couch Potato (A Story About Making Healthy Choices) / Katie Duffield (Changes and Challenges In My Life)
ISBN 978-1-64156-497-7 (hard cover)(alk. paper)
ISBN 978-1-64156-623-0 (soft cover)
ISBN 978-1-64156-734-3 (e-Book)
Library of Congress Control Number: 2018930714

Rourke Educational Media
Printed in the United States of America,
North Mankato, Minnesota

© 2019 Rourke Educational Media

All rights reserved. No part of this book may be reproduced or utilized in any form or by any means, electronic or mechanical including photocopying, recording, or by any information storage and retrieval system without permission in writing from the publisher.

www.rourkeeducationalmedia.com

Edited by: Keli Sipperley
Layout by: Corey Mills
Cover and interior illustrations by: John Joseph